This Little Hippo Book
belongs to

Calum Kennedy

Stumpy's Mill

Tawny Owl
Wood

Spud
Field

Top Acre

Owl
Wood
Meadow

Middle
Field

Stan's
House

Uphill
Field

Riverside
Field

Five Oaks
Field

Marshy Wood

Downhill
Field

Aunt Ellie's
Willow

Whistling
Bridge

River Rib

Wrigglesworth

Beech
Farm

Walter's
Garage

Heron
Wood
Lake

Look out for these other

LITTLE RED
TRACTOR

stories published by Scholastic

The Day of the Big Surprise

The Day of Molehills and Windmills

The Day Auntie Ellie Went for a Swim

Scholastic Children's Books,
Commonwealth House, 1-19 New Oxford Street,
London WC1A 1NU, UK
a division of Scholastic Ltd

London ~ New York ~ Toronto ~ Sydney ~ Auckland
Mexico City ~ New Delhi ~ Hong Kong

First published by Little Hippo, an imprint of Scholastic Ltd, 1999

Text copyright © Peter Tye, 1999
Illustrations copyright © Little Red Tractor Projects Ltd, 1999

ISBN 0 590 54465 9

Printed in China

LITTLE RED

TRACTOR

The Day Stan's World
Turned Upside Down

Story by Peter Tye

Based on the original characters and stories
created by Colin Reeder

Little
Hippo

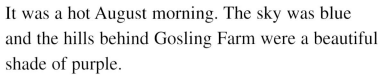

It was a hot August morning. The sky was blue and the hills behind Gosling Farm were a beautiful shade of purple.

In Top Acre Field, the golden wheat swayed gently in the breeze. Stan picked some and rubbed the grain in the palm of his hands.

"It's ready, Patch," he said. "Let's phone Mr Jones!"

Half an hour later, Patch was in the field next
to Little Red Tractor's barn, when she heard
a grumbling sound.

It turned into a loud roar as an enormous yellow
machine came around the corner. It was Mr Jones'
combine harvester. He had arrived to help with
the harvesting.

Mr Jones gave a cheery wave as the chickens rushed squawking into the barn. Stan started Little Red Tractor's engine and they followed Mr Jones and his noisy combine harvester to Top Acre Field.

When they arrived, Stan and Mr Jones had a chat and looked at the wheat. Then Mr Jones set to work.

Rabbits ran from the field to take cover in the hedgerows, as the big yellow machine rumbled through the wheat. Clouds of chaff and dust filled the air.

After a while, Mr Jones waved and Stan drove
Little Red Tractor up beside the yellow combine.
"Keep her steady, Little Red Tractor!" shouted
Stan. Mr Jones pulled a lever and millions of
golden wheat grains poured from the combine into
the trailer.

When the job was finished, Stan and Mr Jones sat down for a glass of lemonade. Stan thanked Mr Jones and, as the great yellow machine lumbered off down the lane, Patch jumped up into Little Red Tractor's cab.

"Move over, Patch," said Stan, as he climbed in beside her. "We've got a lot more work to do."

Back in the yard, Stan shovelled all the grain
into sacks. Next he loaded six sacks on to Little Red
Tractor's trailer.

"Come on, Patch," he said. "We're going up to
Stumpy's Mill."

Stumpy's Mill stood on high ground above Gosling
Farm. On all but the calmest of days, there was
enough wind to turn the great wooden sails.

"Hello, hello," said Stumpy the Miller, with a friendly smile. "What have we here?"

"Six sacks of wheat," said Stan. "Will you grind the wheat into flour please, Stumpy?"

"Right you are," said Stumpy. "First we have to get the sacks up to the top of the mill."

Stumpy lowered the sack lift, as Stan backed Little
Red Tractor's trailer into position. When all the sacks
had been hoisted to the top of the windmill, Stan
climbed the creaking wooden stairs to help Stumpy.

Dust filled the air as they poured the golden grain into the hopper.

"Hang on a moment," said Stumpy, "I'll open the window." But as Stumpy opened the window he got a shock. He saw Rusty, his new kitten, clinging to one of the windmill's sails.

"Rusty!" shouted Stumpy. "Come back in here!"

"I don't think she can," said Stan, "I think she's stuck. Don't worry, Stumpy, I think I can reach her."

Stan clambered out of the window and climbed
along the sail towards Rusty. He stretched out,
gently lifted the kitten off the sail and tucked her
under his arm.

"Got her!" he shouted. Then he paused.
"Er, Stumpy, I think I'm stuck now!"

"Oh no!" said Stumpy. "Hang on tight, Stan. I've got an idea. If I ease the brake off, the sails should go round and take you down to the ground."

Stumpy slowly let the brake off and, with a creak
and a groan, the heavy wooden sails began to turn.

"Help! I'm turning upside down!" shouted Stan. Luckily, as the great sails continued to crank around, he turned the right way up again!

Stumpy gently put the brake back on and ran down the mill staircase three steps at a time. Then he parked Little Red Tractor under the sail. Stan stepped on to the cab and clambered down to the ground. Patch barked loudly at all the excitement.

Stan wiped his brow. "Phew, thank you, Stumpy," he said. "It was quite nasty up there for a moment."

"Well, I think you're very brave, Stan," said Stumpy's wife, Elsie, as she brought out a pot of tea and some biscuits.

After their tea break, they got back to work. The old mill creaked loudly as the giant sails turned in the gentle breeze. Then the massive millstones ground the wheat into flour.

The harvest moon was shining by the time Stan
and Little Red Tractor headed back to Gosling Farm.
It had been a long and exciting day, but Stan had his
feet firmly back on the ground again!

Stumpy's Mill

Tawny Owl
Wood

Spud
Field

Top Acre

Owl
Wood
Meadow

Middle
Field

Stan's
House

Uphill
Field

Riverside
Field

Five Oaks
Field

Marshy Wood

Downhill
Field

Aunt Ellie's
Willow

Whistling
Bridge

River Rib

Wrigglesworth

Beech
Farm

Walter's
Garage

Heron
Wood
Lake